Little
Amazon

Lena Eicher

ISBN: 978-1-936208-36-4

Illustrations by Igor Kondratyuk
Cover design and layout: Kristi Yoder

Printed March 2011
Printed in the USA

Published by:
TGS International
P.O. Box 355 · Berlin, Ohio 44610 USA
Phone: 330-893-4828
Fax: 330-893-2305
www.tgsinternational.com

TGS000352

Table of Contents

Publisher's Note

In an effort to stimulate family interest in foreign missions, the publisher asked the author to write a real-to-life account of a family traveling abroad to visit missionaries. Lena Eicher surpassed our expectations by basing much of the story on her own trip to Belize, but adapting it to a family setting and freely using a writer's liberty. The story of the Muslim man did not actually take place in Belize, although it was drawn from true experiences of Christians who work with Muslims.

CHAPTER 1

Preparing for Belize

The tangerine-tinted sky was just giving way to lemon sun rays that touched gray, wispy clouds, filling the shed with a half light coming through streaked windows. With one hand Franklin pushed bleating lambs away as he moved toward the round water trough and adjusted the hose.

Woolly lambs surrounded him again. He watched them at the trough, catching a reflection of his silhouette in the dark water.

"Today is the day," twelve-year-old Franklin addressed the audience, though they paid no attention to his announcement. "Today we go in for our passports. And I'd rather stay here on our farm than go to Belize." Franklin patted the head of a mother ewe, her lamb crowding her. Bending, he scooped up the lamb and touched the pink nose to the water. *What if something exciting happens here while we're gone? And Barker's supposed to have her puppies.*

Excitement ran high in most of the Van Pelt family. Ever since Daddy had worked with Garth Miller in voluntary service in Belize before he was married, he had planned to someday take his family there. Franklin just wished Daddy would count him out. But nothing Franklin could come up with would persuade Daddy. His mind was made up; they would all go together. *All* meant all five Van Pelts: Daddy Mathias, Mama Annie, Kate, who was fourteen, himself, and nine-year-old Max.

"Daddy, where is Belize on the map?" Franklin had asked.

Daddy had gotten out the globe and showed the family the continent of North America that looked like a kite with Belize on the tail. Belize bordered the south-eastern most edge of Mexico, with Guatemala to the west. "European contact began in 1502," Daddy explained, "when Columbus, likely on his fourth expedition, sailed along the coast."

The first record of the English living in the land was in 1638 by shipwrecked English sailors. Discovering Belize rich with timber, European settlers came, bringing with them African slaves. Because Belize lay along the Caribbean Sea, bands of pirates thrived who ravaged Spanish ships. Britain and Spain fought over the area until the British gained sovereignty in 1802. In 1840, Great Britain formally named it the Colony of British Honduras, but in 1973 the official name changed to Belize.

Daddy had read that Belize City is the largest city in Belize. It lies at the mouth of the Belize River where large ships anchor in port. In 1961, the poorer section of the city was almost wiped out by Hurricane Hattie when it swept ashore October 31.

"That's when the Mennonites came to help," Daddy had explained. "The organizations of Mennonite Disaster Service and Mennonite Central Committee moved in to that storm-ravaged area to provide material aid. Small houses were built. Clothes, food, and medicine were given out along with the Gospel. As the natives came to the Lord, the need for churches grew, so mission compounds were established in several villages to meet the people's spiritual needs. Over the years the missions grew and expanded. Some staff volunteered service only a year or two, as I did. Garth, however, came while I was there and has chosen to serve in missions for a lifetime."

The invitation from Garth and Rachel to visit Belize had come by e-mail: "The twenty-eighth of December would be an excellent time to arrive. Colin is already ecstatic that a boy his age is coming."

Chores finished, Franklin headed toward the house for a

quick breakfast and family devotions. An hour later, the Van Pelts were on their way. Arriving at the town square, Daddy parked the car and the whole family piled out.

Franklin figured the Tyler County Courthouse must have nearly one hundred steps to the front door. He managed to stay in front of the rest of the family, putting one leather-booted foot ahead of the other on the leaf-strewn marble. Kate and Max followed right behind him. Glancing back, he noticed Mama's rosy cheeks and Daddy reaching for her hand to help her along.

Entering the massive building, they found themselves in a large foyer. Their footsteps echoed loudly as they crossed the tile floor to a window where a clerk directed them to the passport office.

As always, Franklin wanted to know all the details. He stood at Daddy's elbow, watching him fill out the long forms. First and Last Name . . . Permanent Address . . . Date of Birth . . . Hair Color . . . Eye Color . . . Social Security Number . . . Occupation . . . Travel Plans . . .

After Daddy completed his own form, he filled out a form for each of his children. Mama was standing by with all their paperwork to help him when he didn't know the answers. When the forms were finished, Mama attached each of their passport pictures into the squares provided.

Leaving the courthouse, they went to the library where Daddy ordered tickets online for a family of five traveling to

Belize and staying eight days.

What will happen on the farm in eight days? Franklin wondered. *Will Brian Carey remember to feed the birds and watch Barker every day? The cows need hay and feed, and the calves need their bottles fixed just right. And does Brian know anything about lambs?*

"Daddy, why do you want me to go along to Belize?" Franklin asked after Daddy turned from the computer. "What if I won't like it?"

Daddy's expression became thoughtful, and as was his habit, he began running his fingers upward through his dark beard. "Poor children who live in that country do not have the advantages you have in the U.S. You need to see them. When you see a Third World culture, you learn to be grateful.

"There's another, a bigger reason for you to discover. I'll give you only a hint. It will be a magnet that will draw you closer to God. You've already given your heart to Jesus, Franklin. Someday He may call you to serve Him at a Third World mission. Before you go, you need to learn His ways."

Daddy's answer gave Franklin a lot to think about. *All my life my parents have taught me about God in the Bible. But I don't really know how He works today.*

Within three weeks the passports came. Five shiny, navy blue booklets, each with a family member's picture and personal information inside.

Franklin eyed his passport photo and wished he had

smoothed down his cow lick. Maybe with five Van Pelts to check in, the ticket agent wouldn't look too closely at his picture. Franklin snapped the book shut and decided to forget it.

"We must keep the passports in a safe place," Mama said, consulting one of her many lists she had lying around. She had lists for everything—jobs for neighbor Brian while the family was away, clothes to be packed in the suitcases which would be checked in at the service counter, items to be packed in the carry-on bags, a list of first aid items, a regular shopping list, and some groceries the missionaries couldn't easily find in Belize. Mama had e-mailed them for a list. Franklin placed the passports into the fire safe where they'd be ready to go when all the things on Mama's lists had been checked off.

Day by day the suitcases were filled. The airline allowed fifty pounds per bag and two check-in bags per person. Each passenger was allowed one carry-on bag of forty pounds and a purse or briefcase. Mama was careful to take only the minimum of what the family needed because they had to allow for the weight of the extra missionary supplies.

Two days after Christmas Mama checked her lists for the last time. ". . . insect repellent, stomach medicines, sandals, sunglasses, mosquito netting, and snacks," she finished reading.

"They're all here, Mama," Franklin said, finding each item in the suitcases.

"Everything is accounted for. Let's hope we don't get those four inches of snow they're predicting by tomorrow morning."

Now excitement ran at a feverish pitch. In spite of having to leave the farm, Franklin couldn't help but catch the spirit too. He crawled into bed soon after nine as Mama insisted, but he just wanted to wiggle. Tomorrow would be the first time he would fly in a jet.

In the frosty darkness of late December, the family loaded their van and were on their way to the Pittsburgh airport by 3:20 a.m. The drive to the airport would take two hours, and they needed to be at the airport for check-in two hours before flight time.

Franklin let his gaze take in the huge interior of the airport while they waited in the check-in line: the dome ceiling, chandelier, attendants in uniform rushing along, and pools of luggage around waiting passengers. His ears rang with the announcements that crackled over the intercom. He eased his backpack to the floor.

Through the window he noticed a lady carrying her poodle in her arms and his thoughts leapfrogged home to his little cocker spaniel. *I sure hope Brian takes time to brush Barker when he feeds her . . . wish I could be there when she has her puppies. I bet she'll miss me 'cause no one takes as good care of her as I do.*

The luggage was checked in. It was time to go through security. Daddy led the way to a large room where people were lined up in front of what appeared to be narrow doorways without doors. Metal detectors, Daddy called them.

Soon the Van Pelts' turn came. An attendant ordered them to place all purses, briefcases, shoes, carry-on luggage, and any items from their pockets on a conveyor belt near one of the metal detectors. Franklin set his backpack on the belt and emptied his pockets—his silver watch and chain, a blue plastic pen, and his red hanky. Attendants peered closely at the X-ray screen for any questionable items passing through.

Franklin watched Mama step through the metal detector. *Beep! Beep!* Her hairpins had set off the beeper. A uniformed lady drew her aside to poke her long, bony fingers into Mama's hair bun under the white veiling. Using a wand, the attendant waved it up and down the entire length of Mama's body. The wand did not beep, so Mama was free to go.

Now it was Franklin's turn. *Beep! Beep!* Franklin winced. He stepped away from the doorway, slapping his pockets. *Now what did I forget to put on the belt?*

"This way, young man." The bony fingers beckoned to him. "Dig deep. What do you have hidden in those pockets, sonny?"

Franklin's fingers grasped something hard. His heart sank even as he drew out the offending pocket knife. *No. I don't*

want to part with this. I bought it after I sold the first litter of Barker's puppies.

"Sorry. It's got to go. Can't go on the plane."

Franklin held on for one more second before dropping the silver treasure into the deep bin beside the belt. He heard it clank.

At the gate waiting area, the Van Pelts watched through the cold winter dawn as huge jets nosed about like fat, white penguins on little feet. Franklin was fascinated. *Just soon we'll get in one of those and go screaming away and become only a speck up in the sky. Only people won't be able to see us because of the snow clouds.* He felt just a little sorry. *If ever I wished someone could see us, it's now. I guess it's not so hard leaving the farm after all if we get to fly.*

At last the voice over the intercom said that US Air flight 756 was now boarding. All the passengers gathered their luggage and formed an orderly line. One by one the gate attendant checked their tickets and passports. Franklin followed a young woman in a bright red blazer, tinted blue hair, and long, dangling ear rings.

Away they hustled, shoulder bags clutched to their sides, down the Jetway and onto the waiting plane. Two flight attendants in crisp uniforms greeted them as they entered. One of them checked Franklin's boarding pass.

"25A, honey," she said, pointing. "Through the curtain and toward the back."

The plane was like a huge, fancy bus. A short hallway

opened into the first class section, an extravagant room with plush blue recliners and tables side by side. The ceiling curved down to form the walls on each side, which had a row of small, oval windows.

From first class, Franklin slipped through the blue curtain into the larger cabin. A sea of seats met his eyes—three seats on either side of the aisle all the way to the back! Above the seats were bins to hold belongings. Each seat had a letter and a number. Franklin looked at his boarding pass again and made his way back through the plane until he found 25A. It was a window seat!

The Van Pelts would sit behind the wing. Stowing their luggage overhead, Daddy and Mama settled into their seats ahead of Franklin, Max, and Kate. Kate unfolded the small lap table in front of Max to show him how to use it.

"Hey, this is neat. Just like a school desk!" he said, pushing it up and down.

A pocket in front of Franklin held travel catalogs and magazines. Picking one out, he flipped through the colorful, glossy pages. He put it back. Another folder gave instructions what to do in case of an emergency. His seat cushion could be used as a float in case they had to land in water. Franklin snapped that one shut and stuck it back into the pocket. *Scary thought. We'd better not have to land in water!*

Gazing out the window, Franklin couldn't get enough of watching the planes. Big birds, small birds, stiff and sleek, all meant for traveling the skies. *Sky ways instead of highways.* He liked that. And the pilots knew the routes even when there weren't any signs.

The pilot's voice came through the intercom overhead. "Welcome aboard US Air. The temperature in Miami is a balmy 78 degrees and it's sunny . . ."

They have summer down in Florida . . . weird for December, ran Franklin's thoughts.

The plane started to roll backward from the gate. A flight attendant opened the folder and began explaining procedures to follow in case of an emergency. Franklin stared out the window, not wanting to miss anything on the outside. The plane turned and lumbered down the long taxiway, coming to a stop at the crossover to the runway. On the adjacent runway an American Airlines jet sped along, nosed into the air, and lifted effortlessly. Franklin watched until it became only a silver speck in the sky.

Bump. Bump. The plane was rolling again. It paused, moved again. The plane turned the last corner, the enormous wings making a wide, sweeping arc. They were in position for takeoff! The pilot gave the engines full throttle, and Franklin felt sucked into his seat as the plane thrust forward. Faster and faster they zoomed. The airport flashed by the window. Other jets. The airfield. Franklin had never known such speed. The front of the cabin rose. The bumping gave way to smoothness. Outside the window the ground fell quickly away. They soared over trees, power lines, and rooftops. Cars, like colored insects, ran along highways that quickly changed from narrow ribbons to pencil lines. *This is what it must feel like to be God and look down on the world,* Franklin thought.

Far away, block-patterned fields became shrouded by the wispy clouds they were passing through. If Franklin could have opened the window, he would have run his arm through one. Then they broke through to an enormous blue sky. Sunshine! Now they were flying above the clouds. Below, as far as eye could see was a bed of cotton.

After the plane was at its cruising altitude of 33,000 feet, the flight attendants served beverages and a snack. Franklin could hardly believe it when the pilot announced they were approaching Miami and the plane started slowly descending. The two hours had passed quickly. He watched as the buildings and cars got bigger and bigger, and then he heard a *snap* as the wheels came down and locked into place. The ground seemed to rise to meet them, and with a bump, the wheels hit the runway. Franklin braced himself with his hand on the seat ahead, feeling the hard brake of the plane.

The Van Pelts changed planes in Miami. Franklin liked this huge, busy airport even more than Pittsburgh. Planes landed and took off constantly. He could have spent hours here just watching them, but they had only enough time for a quick lunch before they had to find their gate and board another plane.

Again the pilot's voice came over the plane's intercom.

"Welcome to Belize Air. We'll have sunshine crossing into Central America today. We should arrive at Belize City in two hours and thirty minutes. The temperature there is 89 degrees. Enjoy the flight and thanks for flying Belize Air."

After reaching cruising altitude, the flight attendants passed out customs forms that everyone needed to fill out before entering a new country. Franklin was glad his father would fill out the one form needed for their family.

Once more the plane descended and circled to land. Franklin took in the scene below. They were flying over a swampy marshland dotted with trees and brush, so different from the wintry land of the north. *So this is Belize. What a different place this is compared to the United States. I don't like swamps and strange people. What could be more exciting here than on the farm?* Franklin did not guess that for him the secret did not lie in Belize City, but way back in the bush along a river called Little Amazon.

CHAPTER 2

Crisis at Tampico

O utside on the observation deck, ladies in white veils and long dresses, and a tall, white-haired man waved. Beside the man stood a blond-haired boy of about nine.

"It's them!" Max launched himself across Franklin to frantically wave from the plane window. "Look, Kate. It's Garth and Rachel." He smacked the window. "Mom, Mom, I think I see Colin climbing up on the rail. Let's get outta here. Hurry!"

"I can't see a thing with your head in the way," Kate complained.

"You're squashing me, Max," Franklin said, strong-arming his brother back into his seat. The seat belt sign was turned off. Passengers started gathering their bags.

"Let's get outta here. Hurry!" Max insisted.

Franklin grabbed Max's shirt collar just before he darted into the crowded aisle. "Hold up, Max. We have to take our stuff."

Daddy handed bags down to Mama, Franklin, and Kate. The lightest one he handed to Max. When all the luggage was

accounted for, the Van Pelts moved with the rest of the passengers down the aisle and through the open door into warm
tropical sunshine. A stairway led down to the tarmac.

Inside the plain block building, Franklin was surprised at
how small and ordinary things looked in this airport. "Low-
key," Daddy would say. At the counter they showed their
passports to the immigration officials who stamped them and
added their fancy signatures.

Franklin was intrigued with the conveyor belt. Luggage
came through a hole in the outside wall and moved around
and around until someone claimed it.

"That's our suitcase," Max exclaimed when a green suitcase
popped through the hole.

"I'll get Mama and Daddy's blue one," said Franklin, grab-
bing the handle and lifting the suitcase off the belt.

The uniformed men at customs checked the family's luggage. Daddy talked them into lowering duty fees for some of
their possessions because Garth had warned him about not
allowing the agents to take advantage.

Outside the secure area, Franklin felt a hand on his shoulder. He looked up. "Rachel?"

"Mathias! Annie! Welcome to Belize." The pleasant-faced,
tall woman met them with outstretched arms. The men were
laughing and vigorously shaking each other's hands. Garth
and Daddy had been good friends in the bush years ago.

Two girls who didn't look as if they belonged to Garth's

family amiably chatted with Kate about the trip. They must be two of the voluntary service workers helping out at the mission.

In time the luggage was loaded onto the Toyota van. Garth and Daddy would do the driving. The rest piled in, Belizean style, the youngest sitting on laps.

Fascinated, Franklin peered out through the van window. Odd strings of Christmas lights decorated small shops that sold anything from hubcaps to bright little dresses and hanging meats. Flies crawled over the meat. Orange taxis honked their way along the street, nosing in and out of a crowd of dark-skinned people on bicycles threading their way among the cars and buses that left noxious trailing plumes of smoke. Music blared from a tavern where several men in bright shirts and ragged pants stood around smoking.

Expertly, Garth maneuvered the van through the crush until at last they turned in the lane at Gospel Light Christian Mission. The van doors flew open. Pungent, sweet smoke from a cigarette wafted over the compound's tall wooden fence and assaulted Franklin's nostrils.

"Come inside and get comfortable," Garth spoke in his great booming voice. "Rachel, I'm sure these folks would enjoy a drink."

❊ ❊ ❊ ❊ ❊ ❊ ❊ ❊ ❊ ❊ ❊ ❊ ❊ ❊ ❊ ❊ ❊ ❊

"Is the mission back in Little Amazon doing well?" Daddy asked Garth the next morning after breakfast. "I've of-

ten wondered what became of Pedro and his family after his mother died of those burns."

"You'll see for yourself when we travel back to the clinic today. Pedro is pastoring the Little Amazon mission church after spending five years in the States attending Bible school. He married a fine young lady, and they have two little boys."

"I want to see Pedro again. And hear Kekchi by those Indians."

"What is Kekchi, Daddy?"

"I'll let Garth tell you, son. He's more knowledgeable in the subject."

The big man of the house was rummaging through his desk, gathering materials.

Opening his briefcase, he placed his Bible inside along with a memo pad and binder.

Taking a flashlight from the shelf, he flipped it on and off. "We'll need this back there," he said to no one in particular, tucking it absently into a corner of the briefcase. "Kekchi? You want to know about Kekchi?" Garth turned and gave his guests his full attention.

"Kekchi, one of fifty-plus Mayan languages still spoken in Guatemala today, is more closely related to the Mayan languages of southern Mexico. There are probably 700,000 Kekchi Indians who live in Alta Verapaz in northern Guatemala. A number have settled in Belize and many are migrating to California and New York. They are animistic, which means they believe rocks, trees, and the wind are alive and have souls. They are greatly influenced by the trend to switch back to the old Mayan religion."

"I've heard the Kekchi Bible has had quite an impact," injected Daddy.

"The Kekchi Bible has had a tremendous impact on the Kekchi," Garth agreed. "It resulted in a people's movement in the 1980s when thousands turned to the Lord. The Christians continue on today with a concern for reaching their own people with the Gospel. The Nazarenes, the Southern Baptists, the Mennonites, and various Pentecostal groups are all using the Kekchi Bible and holding their services in the Kekchi language. The people are proud of their culture and language, but still burdened to reach others with the true Gospel message. It is an indigenous work that will continue long after all of us missionaries have left the country."

"Interesting, Garth. So how soon do we leave?"

"As soon as we can get ready. If you remember, it's an all-day trip. From here you have the bunny hop over the jungle to Tampico; then you take the skiff over sea about an hour to the Little Amazon River. Then it's back that way another two hours. Keep in mind, when the sea is rough, it's not for the faint of heart."

"How well I remember," Daddy said thoughtfully. "Once during a storm we nearly lost a few passengers."

At the note in Daddy's voice, Franklin looked up from

watching Rachel weave a basket with quick, sure hands. "You never told us that story."

"I didn't, did I? We'll save it for another time, son. It's all part of the special package benefits of being in the Lord's work in a foreign country. Sometime you'll understand. For now let's get our bags together and head for Little Amazon."

It was decided Rachel would travel along with Garth, but Colin would stay with the other mission couple a block down the street.

Max groaned—his new friend couldn't go along! He had just pulled a shiny new truck from his bag and was offering it to Colin. "I have one just like it. See, you pull on this stick and—see it run?" Max scooted across the wooden floor, chasing after the toy. "It just doesn't fly as fast as that jet did yesterday," he said.

Mama assigned luggage to each family member so nothing would be left behind.

Back at the airport, the Van Pelts had a two-hour wait. "They're doing maintenance on the plane," Daddy informed the family after returning from the ticket counter.

"It's gonna take so long," Max complained. "And there aren't even planes here to watch like in Miami."

"That's because we're in Belize now," Kate reminded him. "Things don't work here like they do in the States. Why don't you settle down and read a book?"

"Because I didn't bring a book. I came to see the monkeys."

Mama looked up from the word search book on her lap. "Here, Max. Help me find the names of insects in this box."

Franklin couldn't settle down to anything. All he wanted was to get going, over the treetops and far away. It was just too bad to be stuck in a dingy airport on such a sunny day.

At last they were airborne. Everything about the trip fascinated Franklin, from the plane's bright fourteen-seat interior to the instrument panel with all its buttons and dials to the lush green jungle speeding by beneath their wings. *I hope the pilot knows what he's doing, flying so low,* he thought to himself.

A red dirt track cut through the bush. A landing strip? Sure enough.

The plane circled and all the passengers held on to their seats as the plane bumped to a stop beside a lone woman waiting with her suitcase. No buildings were in sight. As soon as she climbed aboard, they were off again.

I wonder what happens if there's an emergency out here, Franklin's thoughts ran. *Say somebody has a heart attack or the plane motor catches on fire. There'd be no way fire trucks could get through this bush.*

At Tampico the plane banked, descended, and hit another dirt track that led to a weathered shed that served as the town's airport.

"Here's where we get off," Garth instructed them. "The boat dock is only a few blocks away. We'll put your luggage on the mission van from here. There's business I need to take care of. Then we'll leave for Little Amazon once everything is wrapped up."

Gathering their belongings, the Van Pelts, Garth, and Rachel disembarked and loaded their luggage onto the white van in the parking lot. "There's a good little restaurant just a few blocks away in town. I'll take you there and while you eat, I'll have a tire on this van changed," Garth said. Behind them the plane roared and took off again. Franklin watched it climb up into the sky, the noon sun glinting off its wings.

They had just started bumping over the rutted street toward the restaurant when Mama let out a cry. Her face went completely white. "Oh, Mathias! My purse. My purse is gone!" Hunched down in the seat, she groped frantically in the space on the floor where her purse should have been.

"Annie," Daddy's hand stopped in midair on its way down from ruffling Max's hair. "Did you leave it in Belize City?" he asked, alarmed.

"No!" she wailed. "I know I had it on my shoulder when we got onto the plane. I must've left it under the seat. Oh, Mathias, I'm so sorry!"

Franklin felt the wash of a chill as if a bucket of slush had been dumped on him. *All our tickets! Our passports. Everything is stored in Mama's purse. I put them there myself for safekeeping. They're gone. We'll never get that purse back.*

CHAPTER 3

One Against a Thousand

The van lurched to a stop under a scraggly shade tree where chickens scratched around in the dirt. "Let's go back," Garth said. In nearly one motion, he whipped the van around and they were headed back to the airport. "We'll radio the plane right away. Maybe the pilot can save the purse before someone takes it."

Maybe. Franklin distinctly remembered seeing five passengers board the plane before it took off again.

While Garth talked to the airport attendant, the group outside formed a circle in the shade and prayed.

Only Max and Kate seemed to enjoy the rice and beans, Ricardo chicken, and Fanta drink Daddy ordered at the small blue building with a screened-in porch. Though Franklin put on a show of eating, he watched Daddy only pick at his food and knew he was worried. Once he spoke across the picnic tables to Daddy, but Daddy didn't hear. He just stared at a huge leafy bush that shaded the cook house, knit his brows, and again and again ran his fingers up through his beard. He massaged the back of his neck. Mama didn't eat at all, but instead sat white and still in the warm tropical afternoon.

Will God answer our prayers? Franklin's mind teased the thought like a kitty playing with her tail. He couldn't let it go. *The natives will have fun using our credit cards.*

After lunch, the quiet group found the garage where Garth was bent over a wheel, working with the tire. Grease and sweat stained his friendly face. His white shirt was soaked through.

"Can I help you there, Garth?" Daddy offered. "Looks like we came just in time."

"I won't turn down an extra pair of hands." Garth grunted and heaved the wheel over to the jacked-up rear of the van. "Grab hold." Together the men lifted the wheel and fitted it into place. Garth started the lug nuts and Daddy worked the wrench. The hub cap made a tinny sound as it snapped into place.

"I have a few more errands," Garth said when he straightened to his full height of nearly six feet. "You can walk down to the pier where we get the skiff." He traced directions for them in the hot air with his thick finger. "The airport said they got in touch with the pilot and they found the purse. I suppose it's okay to be cautiously optimistic."

A cheer went up around Franklin. "They found the purse! They found the purse!" Kate sang. Carefully Franklin kept his gaze on the ground, his sandal forming a tiny wall of powdery dirt. *No one is mentioning that the purse could be empty.* Franklin refused to look at Mama. He could hardly bear to see her pain, the way she was nearly shriveled up from the stress just in the hours since the discovery. *I don't think for Mama's sake I could bear it if the purse came back empty.*

The road to the pier led past shacks the size of chicken coops back home. Some had curtained, screenless windows. Some were like garden sheds. Flowers adorned window boxes here and there. Rags and junk lay scattered. Children and animals scrounged in the dirt around the doorways. Friendly voices called out Spanish greetings to the passersby. Through leafy trees the shimmer of ocean blue came into view.

"Daddy." Franklin's worries had finally taken audible shape. They walked side by side, the rest moving ahead. "How can we be sure God will give back the purse? Full? With everything in it?"

"We can't be sure. We just ask Him and trust Him to act. And often, I've noticed, the more specifically we pray, the more specifically God answers."

"What if the answer is no?" Franklin reached out and grabbed a leaf on a bush.

The stem broke and he heard the branch snap back into place.

"God will do whatever gets Him the most glory. We should always ask God to glorify Himself."

"But if the stuff inside is lost?"

"Then we'll ask God what He wants us to do next."

"Oh, Daddy, it would be so much work! It would probably take the rest of the trip to get all the paperwork together again to go home, wouldn't it?"

"Maybe. It would mean ordering new passports from the embassy, which could take several days' work, canceling the credit cards we brought along, calling the airport for new tickets, and canceling the cell phone. When we get home, Mama would need to order a new driver's license . . ."

"Daddy, stop. It would be so much easier if God would just protect everything."

"We're thankful Mama put most of the cash in our carry-on bag. We still have that."

"What do you think God will do?" Franklin was back at the original question. Kitty chasing her tail.

"If you study the ways of God in the Old Testament, it seems God's favorite ratio is 1 to 1,000."

"What do you mean, Daddy?"

"Take Gideon, for example. It wasn't until his army was reduced to an insignificant number that God used them to go against the thousands of Midianites. Samson was one against a horde and he brought down the house. David was only one when he faced Goliath with his Philistine army behind him. God is most interested that we are not strong in ourselves.

"Often God takes everything from us till we are so small there's not a chance we can match our challenger alone. Then, when we are most helpless, God shows his greatest strength. So *He* gets *all* the glory." They walked along in silence.

Overhead, the whine of an approaching plane grew louder,

causing Daddy and Franklin to look skyward. A long body of black and silver flew over their heads and circled just above the treetops. "That's him!" Franklin shouted, breaking into a run in the direction of the airstrip, Daddy following close behind at a sprint. They turned the last corner.

Outside the shed someone waved—Mama. She had made it ahead of them and in her upraised hands, waving it aloft by the shoulder strap, was her big, beautiful emerald purse! In a minute they closed the gap between them.

"Is everything there?" Franklin asked in one breath.

"Annie, the passports?" was all Daddy could say, heaving for breath after the sprint.

"Here, see for yourself!" Mama said in wonderment, handing the purse to Daddy who grabbed it and dug through the contents. Franklin watched his fingers count five shiny navy passports. The tickets were also in their respective envelopes. The credit cards were undisturbed. Franklin felt his knees buckle with relief.

"Dear God, thank you!" Daddy sang out under his breath. "Let's go find the others. They'll want to know."

The entire group celebrated by the sea, thanking God for so wonderfully protecting the purse and returning it safely to the Van Pelts. As nearly as could be determined, not one penny was missing. All had been safely restored. The passports, the tickets, the credit cards, and cell phone. Nothing had been abused or lost.

✳ ✳ ✳ ✳ ✳ ✳ ✳ ✳ ✳ ✳ ✳ ✳ ✳ ✳ ✳ ✳ ✳ ✳ ✳

It was 3 p.m. Rarely did the skiff leave that late for the three-hour trip back to the bush. The luggage and village supplies were loaded and covered with a large blue tarp in the middle of the skiff, making the pile look like a mountain separating the passengers as they piled on. Daddy and Garth were in the back with the boys, and the girls and women were sitting in the front. It would probably be dark by the time they arrived at Little Amazon village.

The rope fastening the skiff to the pier was untied. The motor roared and away they skimmed across the sea. Franklin gazed over the quiet mirror of water so close to the edge of the boat and marveled that this crowd of people traveled safely only inches from what could be their death. No one had the luxury of life jackets. Maybe a strong swimmer could make it if the skiff capsized, for never during the journey did they lose sight of land.

Franklin found himself seated beside a slight, weathered old man with penetrating eyes, who spoke precise English. All the way across the sea Franklin felt the man watching him, scrutinizing these American visitors.

They entered the mouth of the Little Amazon. Lined with trees, the river flowed through the dense jungle like a silent ribbon of brown. Light from the bright afternoon changed to dusk. Several times the pilot of the skiff stopped to attend to one of the sputtering motors.

The beauty of untamed nature in the tropical forest fascinated Franklin. A lizard clung half way up the trunk of a tree. Somewhere a woodpecker tap-tatted away. House plants, like the ones at home, grew tall as trees. One bush was bursting with large pink flowers. Brightly colored birds chattered, and behind all this cacophony, Franklin could hear the scream of monkeys in the treetops.

"This man, Mathias Van Pelt, he is your father?" the old man ventured.

"Yes," Franklin answered over the noise of the motors, wondering that the man had picked up on the full name. "We are only here for a visit to the village."

"Ah."

"Do you live at Little Amazon?" Franklin cast about for something to say.

"The next village farther up the trail."

When the wooden seat under Franklin became hard and no position was comfortable anymore, at last through growing darkness he made out the shapes of grass huts high on the bank to their left. They had arrived. This was their destination, Little Amazon village. There was no sign to announce it, only a crowd of silhouettes gathered on the bank.

There was no dock at which to tie the skiff. The driver nosed it up to rest in mud. The supplies from under the tarp were passed to willing hands who carried them up to the mission house. The skiff passengers scrambled up over gnarled tree

roots to the top of the bank. Before them spread a charming village of bamboo huts.

The old man had grabbed a walking stick and now stood at Franklin's elbow.

"Come to my village, San Jose, and ask for Xavier ('zāv-yər) Clemente. Come soon. Don't go home until I have talked to your father." Franklin did not miss the urgency in the strange man's voice.

"I will tell him. But Pedro lives in the village. I heard Garth say he visits folks."

"No, no. Tell your father he must come. He is the one I saw in the dream."

Franklin started after the man but lost him in the darkness and the crowd. The path led over open meadow to the mission compound, where the Van Pelts stowed their suitcases in the guesthouse and then went to Pedro's house for supper. The weary party entered through the gate and moved up the wooden steps under bamboo thatch to the front porch.

They entered a large, spacious house, designed to allow maximum airflow in the tropical heat. The open, unscreened windows upstairs had wooden shutters, while the lower level windows were screened and covered with heavy wire to keep out insects as well as intruders.

By dim, solar-powered light, the hungry travelers devoured a supper of rice and beans. When Pedro lit the propane gas lantern, it really brightened the room.

Over and over the old man's face floated through Franklin's weary brain. *What does he want with Daddy? He recognized him from a dream? Strange. I'll tell Daddy when I get a chance.*

Daddy looked exhausted after supper. Kate could hardly contain her yawns, and Max had fallen asleep with his head on Mama's lap. Elena, Pedro's gentle wife, suggested they all go to bed and wait to visit until morning.

The guest hut had two bedrooms, each with a set of bunk beds, and a bathroom the size of a small closet. The boys would sleep in the back room and Kate in the front one. Mama and Daddy stayed in the big house. By light of kerosene lamps and flashlights, they all prepared for bed. In minutes Franklin had settled in the bottom bunk and fallen fast asleep. In his dreams an old, wizened man held out his arm, beckoning him to come.

CHAPTER 4

Franklin Solves a Problem

The next morning Franklin awoke to a humid, sunny day. The family was greeted at the mission house by village ladies intent on selling their crafts. Mama bought a colorful tortilla cloth and two small dollies she said would make nice gifts.

"Come and have breakfast," Elena invited her guests. She laid out a spread on the picnic table under a thatch-roofed pavilion behind the guesthouse. "This will be your dining room," she said.

Franklin felt surrounded by beauty. The low thatch roof of the guesthouse hung down, nearly touching a trimmed, flowering hedge that stretched over to the far corner where a red outhouse stood. To the left spread an expansive lawn dotted with banana trees of various heights. Beyond the grove fence on the far side was open meadow, and in the middle, the bamboo church building.

Pedro's family had already eaten breakfast in the big house. While the Van Pelts, Garth, and Rachel ate a breakfast of cornflakes and cinnamon rolls without icing, Franklin noticed a pig rooting in the thick undergrowth behind an old, rickety wire fence. In the compound lawn to their right, he noticed a thatch-roofed, wire-walled chicken coop. After spooning in the last bite of cornflakes, he ran to help feed the white chicks and fat, brown laying hens.

The old man said he lives in the village beyond this one, Franklin remembered, his gaze searching the jungle beyond the clearing. *What does the man want that is so urgent? I didn't get a chance to tell Daddy. If Pedro hadn't come right after breakfast and called him and Garth to help take the supplies to the clinic, I could have.*

After the chores, Tito and Miguel, two boys about Franklin's age, offered to give Franklin, Max, and Kate a tour of the village. Mama accompanied them to the only hut with a telephone, where she made a call home. In this very damp but pleasant, breezy weather, it was hard to believe the temperature at home was two degrees below zero.

Leaving Mama at the telephone hut, Franklin and Kate followed Miguel and Tito to the wood carver's house. Diego wasn't home so Tito suggested they call on Diego's brother Antonio.

To get there, the path led down a hill into a swampy bottom where boards were laid across the soggy ground. On the opposite side the hill rose steeply. At the top stood Antonio's hut.

Antonio greeted them with a smile and a warm handshake,

invited them in, and had them sit on benches. At the moment, he was carving a cup out of beautiful rosewood, so they watched him for some time while they visited.

Finally Tito told him why they had come. "The American visitors would like to see your collection of carvings."

Antonio gladly showed them his treasures of rosewood: smooth crosses, matching hearts, a skiff with a paddle, and a tortilla bowl on a tray. All were made of the same beautiful rosewood.

"Rosewood," Antonio explained, "comes from hardwood trees and is an ornamental wood like this." He picked up a dark red and purplish-colored cross streaked with black. "This oily, fragrant wood is very durable. It comes from the purplish black heartwood of old trees. In the U.S. you might see rosewood used whole or in veneer for piano casings or other cabinet work. It's been used for hundreds of years but is now nearly extinct. The oil from the wood and leaves is used in perfumes and soaps. Rosewood is also a substitute for ebony."

Kate asked to buy the tray from the collection and the cup Antonio was working on. Franklin decided on the skiff and paddle.

"Once I have a nice supply of carvings, I take them to market. There are a few good markets here in Belize and in Guatemala where tourists come. Xavier Clemente from the next village sells his hammocks and carvings at the same place."

"You know Xavier then." It was a statement more than a

question. "He seems to know my father," Franklin explained. "Xavier wants Daddy to visit before we leave Little Amazon."

A strange, tight expression Franklin couldn't read crossed the handsome dark features of the Belizean. Then, ignoring his guests, Antonio turned and started carrying the carvings back behind the curtain where he stored them.

Abruptly the visit was over. Antonio said they could pay for their carvings when the cup was finished. He escorted them to the door. Again they were out on the sun-soaked path back to the mission.

"Well, what do you make of that?" Kate spoke in undertones, sliding down the bank ahead of her brother.

Franklin's feet hit the wooden boards. "Odd, I'd say. Something's eating him."

At the mission Franklin was drafted to help dry dishes after lunch—dishes that had been washed in cold water. *There sure are some strange things that go with missionary life,* he mused, turning a plate over and over in his hands. The yellow roses were nearly worn off.

He followed Daddy and Pedro, who had volunteered to help the natives thatch a roof. Garth had gone with others downriver on the skiff to bring back cahoon palm leaves. Franklin watched them take a leaf and bind the small separate parts together and arrange them neatly to form a very waterproof roof.

Before they finished, Franklin left. With nothing else to do, he trailed Mama and Elena, who were visiting village homes.

In Little Amazon the homes often consisted of two huts, one for cooking and one for sleeping. Natives slept in hammocks suspended from overhead beams. Sometimes through the day hammocks were knotted up so they were out of the way. Clothes were hung on a clothesline strung across the room.

Cooking utensils hung from nails on the wall. Lids were placed in a wire rack. Franklin and the ladies watched Marta, the lady of one home, kneel on the earthen floor and make corn tortillas. She had cooked the corn for a long time, cooled it, and then put it through a mill. On a tortilla stone she ground it even finer.

A toddler wearing only a dirty blue shirt wandered into the hut, followed by a grunting pig. Marta ignored both.

When the grinding was finished, she shaped and baked the tortillas over an open fire burning in the low stone hearth. Franklin watched the whole process, fascinated.

"The things we eat most," Marta said in answer to Mama's question, "are rice and beans and tortillas, chicken, and plantain."

Watching two scrawny chickens pecking away along the inside wall, Franklin wondered how much meat you could get off their bones. About then a skinny, yellow dog stalked into the hut. The chickens, not to be cheated, pursued their lunch, but the pig, sensing it was no longer welcome, trotted back outside.

After Marta fried a stack of tortillas, she filled a pot with plantain and put it over the fire to boil.

"Plantain is a kind of banana that can be used at all stages of ripeness," she explained, wiping her fingers on her flowered skirt. "Most times it has to be cooked. Only very ripe plantain is eaten raw. It is usually more firm than banana and not as sweet. My husband tells me plantain is a staple food in this country, much like the potato is in the United States. It feels and tastes somewhat the same."

In the homes they visited, they were offered Kool-Aid, Nestea, and Cocoa, a chocolate drink that Franklin thought tasted sandy. It seemed strange to see primitive huts with a clock on the wall and a radio on a small table. Calendars were also very popular.

He glanced at the calendar, noticing that tomorrow night was New Year's Eve.

The evening church service started at five. The church building had a tin roof and cement floor, but the walls were weathered bamboo sticks. When people walked by, Franklin could see their shapes through the walls. A large blackboard hung on the

47

wall behind the podium, and on either side of the blackboard hung a motto. The words on the mottoes were not English, so Franklin could not read them.

Among the handful of natives who sat on rough wooden benches, Franklin searched for the old grizzled man Xavier from the next village. He was not among them. *I must tell Daddy tonight. Surely I'll get a chance when we get home from church.*

The natives who had gathered sang familiar tunes, but with Kekchi words. Franklin hummed along. When the service had started, only a few natives were in attendance besides Pedro and his family and visitors. As the service progressed, more women, children, and men drifted in across the meadow to fill the benches of the church.

Soon it grew dark. Pedro lit an oil lamp before beginning to read. He also lit the overhead gas lantern, but it did little to light the room enough for anyone else to read, even those only a few feet away.

Later, over a supper of mashed potatoes, hot dogs, and sauerkraut, Daddy voiced his concern to Pedro about the need to get the Gospel into people's hearts.

"First of all they need to attend the services to hear the preaching of the Word. They also need to see the Scriptures for themselves. It has always troubled me when a congregation can't follow the preacher because they have no Bibles or they can't read, or it's too dark for them to read."

The conversation turned to other needs of the church in a

village like this. *Imagine having no Bible story books at home. Or all the other Christian stories Mama reads to us at bedtime,* Franklin thought.

All of this was pushed to the back of his mind as they prepared for bed that night. Franklin had just put on his pajamas when, through the open window, he heard the rustling noise of approaching footsteps. Not just one set of footsteps. It sounded like a crowd outside.

Max had the little bathroom door open while he brushed his teeth. With his toothbrush still in his mouth, he turned, eyes large as two fat blueberries, and pointed. "Who is it?" he said around the brush.

Franklin shook his head. "I don't know."

Kate joined him, standing by his elbow. "I heard my name. Ever since we've come, the fellows have been trying to get my attention."

The footsteps stopped under the window. Franklin heard the rustle of clothing and low murmur of voices.

"Mama said to treat the fellows respectfully but don't give them any encouragement. Since Daddy isn't here, Franklin, you'll have to ask them to leave."

Through the window came a low whistle. "Kate! Come out here!"

What would Daddy do? Franklin asked himself. Placing a chair under the window and stepping up on it, he peered outside. By light of the moon, he counted the shadowy shapes of six young boys: Tito and Miguel and four of their friends.

"Hi, boys, you need something?"

"Kate. Get your sister to the window," said a round-faced lad in short pants.

Franklin shook his head. "We have to go to bed. She doesn't want to talk to you."

"Why she no want to talk with me?" a lean fellow said as he moved forward and tapped the screen.

Franklin's face grew hot. *Those boys are just looking for trouble. What can I do?*

Franklin looked down at Kate, only two feet from him in the near darkness. He also noticed something lying on the table.

An idea popped into his brain. "We don't want to keep you if it's your bedtime," he addressed their visitors. "But before you go, how about I read you a story? A bedtime story?"

One of the boys snickered, but Franklin ignored him. Picking up the Bible story book from the table under the window and flipping on the flashlight, he started reading aloud in the circle of light. It was the story of Elijah and the contest on Mt. Carmel. Before Franklin reached the part where the fire fell and burnt up Elijah's sacrifice, the boys scattered into the night.

Franklin turned from the window. "They're gone, Kate," he said. "I guess they don't like bedtime stories."

"Probably never heard any," his sister said, slapping him on his back. "Whatever made you think of it?"

"It just came to me," he shrugged. "Let's get to bed. I'm bushed!"

CHAPTER 5

Earnest 911 Prayers

"Daddy, do you know an old man named Xavier from the next village?"

Finally Franklin had the opportunity to relay the message from the stranger. "He seems to know you and asked you to visit him before we leave here."

"Xavier, Xavier? What else?" Daddy pondered the name.

"Clemente, I think he said. Xavier Clemente."

Daddy shook his head. "I don't recall the name. Still . . . he could remember me from the time Garth and I used to preach in the jungle villages."

"He said you were in his dream."

"Dream? Franklin, I wish you would have told me earlier."

Franklin shrugged. "I wanted to, Daddy. But you and Garth were always so busy. And other times I forgot. You still have time to go, don't you? Before we go home?"

"We'll make time." Daddy studied the banana trees in the yard from the porch of the mission. "Maybe tomorrow, New Year's Day, I can slip over there."

"May I go along, Daddy?"

"I don't see why not. Maybe Pedro could take us, and on the way we could explore the jungle."

"Explore the jungle? Great!"

"I'll talk to Pedro."

Pedro said since Garth and Mathias had helped him with his work, he felt caught up now. He was only glad to return the favor. Tomorrow, it was decided, Garth would man the mission station while Pedro would lead Mathias and Franklin over to San Jose village. They would leave at sunup.

For New Year's Eve, the adults voted to have a prayer circle and fellowship at the mission house. The young folks would play table games at the guesthouse. The idea came from the clinic voluntary service girls. Franklin had met redheaded Kayla and Julie, the short, freckled girl, at the airport, but hadn't run into them since. The girls worked from dawn till evening at the clinic on the far edge of Little Amazon.

When Daddy heard about the young boys at the window the night before, he said he would try to keep an eye on things tonight. "If they bother you, I'll come down. Or you can call for me."

By the light of two flickering oil lamps, Franklin laid out the game of Settlers on the kitchen table. Julie pulled up a chair at his right. Kayla teased Max, hiding the playing pieces under the table as he distributed them so that he lost count.

"Hey, girl! Put those cards up here where I can see them,"

Max commanded, reaching for them and trying to wrestle them out of Kayla's hand.

Kate giggled, joining in the fun. Now both girls were hiding playing pieces under the table and Max scrambled back and forth trying to retrieve them.

Right in the middle of lively laughter, the kitchen doorknob rattled. Kate jumped, a flash of fear crossing her face.

Everyone quieted, listening. The wooden door drifted open. Slowly, Julie got up and crossed the room to the door. "Who's there?" she spoke to the darkness. Franklin heard the lock on the screen door click. When no one spoke, Julie closed and locked the inside door too.

The commotion outside started again. "Kate! Kate!" began the catcalls. Franklin jumped at the noise at the window. A thud. Someone must have thrown something that bounced off the wall. "Whee!" came a whistle. "Let us in!" said an unfamiliar voice.

"Those boys!" Kate exclaimed. "What will we do?"

"Boys? You mean men," Julie said in a worried voice. "They've been drinking."

"Would it help to talk to them?" Franklin asked, laying down two cards of wheat he had been holding. "Or read them a Bible story again?"

"You can't reason with drunk men. Why don't we play, Max?" Kate whispered, trying to keep the others interested in the game. "Let's just ignore them."

As hard as they tried to ignore the distractions outside, concentration became impossible. Finally Kayla went to the door. "I want you to leave!" she addressed the troublemakers. "You're not to be hanging around on the mission compound like this, bothering our guests. If you keep on, I'll need to get Pedro and Garth!"

"Lone white gal for me," said a deep voice so close to the

door Kayla jumped back. "Plenty buay (boys) from di village. You come out. I whan tek yu to Pedro's house."

The man gave an evil laugh. Franklin felt the hair on his arms rise.

"You buy plenty of something you shouldn't," Kayla retorted. "I don't want to go with you. Now you leave!" she repeated. Slamming the door shut, she threw the bolt. A roar of laughter rose from outside. Now there was no pretense of sleuth. Over and over something smacked the wall of the hut. Loud rock music pulsated through the window from a boom box, accompanied by drunken laughter. Before Julie could get to the window to close it, someone blew in a strong, pungent plume of cigarette smoke.

The air felt damp and close with the window shut. Franklin felt he might suffocate. *What can we do? Why doesn't Daddy come down?*

"I wish Garth would hear what's happening out there. Over the noise I heard singing coming from the house," Julie said presently.

By now the game was forgotten.

"I think we should pray," Kayla suggested. "It's getting ugly outside."

As one body they formed a circle. Usually Franklin felt uneasy in a situation like this. He didn't like to pray out loud with strangers in the group, especially with girls. But the urgency of the moment compelled him to forget himself and pray to God for their safety. Even so he hoped he didn't need to say a fancy prayer because he didn't know any. But what was it Daddy had said about God? "When we are most helpless, God shows His greatest power." God could show His power here by sending angels.

Kayla prayed first, followed by Julie and Kate. Finally after a short silence Franklin gulped and plunged in. "Dear Jesus, we're worried about the crowd outside. Would you come and help us? This is my 911 prayer to you . . . from Belize. Send your angels to surround this place. We sure need them now." Another thump rattled a motto on the wall. They jumped as the motto crashed to the floor.

Kate prayed again. "I'm so scared, Lord. What if those men break down the door or rip a screen? They're drunk, God. They don't know what they're doing. Please send your angels."

"Yes, please do, Jesus," Max entreated. Franklin opened one eye just in time to see his brother vigorously nodding his head.

Earnest prayers continued for several more minutes. This time Kayla prayed by name for each fellow whose voice she recognized. Suddenly everything grew quiet outside. *Did they leave?* Franklin wondered. The tension was palpable.

CHAPTER  6

God's Miraculous Answer

At that moment a rustle sounded overhead on the thatch, the sound gathering to a roar. Rain! The Lord had sent rain!

Franklin dashed to the door and yanked it open just in time to see fleeing silhouettes disappear in the downpour. Warm, tropical air greeted his nostrils. The others gathered behind him, exclaiming over the miracle.

"One minute we're begging God for help. The next minute rain is pouring down and all those men are running. God must've just turned on His garden hose!" Max chortled. "Just wait till I tell Daddy and Mama."

"There's a little more water out there than from a hose, silly." Franklin sank down on the sofa to digest it all. *First Mama's purse, now this. God is really close in Belize. How come? I'll have to think about this.*

"I can't believe it! I have to pinch myself." Julie's face shone with excitement. "God is real. And He's here," she said with awe.

Kayla stood in the doorway listening. When she was satisfied all had gone, she turned. "God has so dramatically answered our prayers for help. Wouldn't it be right to thank Him?"

Again the little group formed a prayer ring, this time in praise and worship for the wonderful way God had chosen to answer their prayers.

"I want to go up to the mission house and tell Daddy," Max said when they finished. "Franklin, come with me."

The rain fell steadily. Franklin stood at the door, undecided. "It's dark and muddy out there. I'm sure the men are gone, Max. We'll be okay here."

"We can tell them first thing in the morning," Julie suggested.

"Okay then." Max said, satisfied.

The crisis of the evening played itself out over and over in Franklin's mind as he tried to sleep. He turned this way and that on the narrow bunk. *What if they had broken in? Could Max and I have protected the girls? That was scary. I've never been this close to drunks before.*

After everyone settled in their rooms for the night, Franklin heard a scuffling noise at the door. Thinking someone was trying to get in again, he said in a loud voice, "Keep out!" The hair on his arms stood on end as he lay crouched, tense.

A feminine giggle came across the shaft of light now cast by the moon. "Franklin, relax! It's just me," Kayla whispered. "I remembered the door wasn't barred so I tried to sneak over here without anyone hearing me."

58

Franklin groaned. "Next time make a lot of noise," he said into his pillow. "Please!"

❉ ❉ ❉ ❉ ❉ ❉ ❉ ❉ ❉ ❉ ❉ ❉ ❉ ❉ ❉ ❉ ❉ ❉

At first the narrow trail on which Pedro led Mathias and Franklin took them through high brush; then the brush became low jungle. In a maroon shirt and long gray pants, with a wicked-looking machete hanging from his belt, Pedro looked prepared to take on anything. In his muscular hand he carried a thick walking stick.

After a short fifteen-minute tramp, they came to the "jungle highway." Franklin thought that on the farm at home this would have been a field lane. The path had been slightly muddy till now. But this lane was rutted, rocky, and slick in many places with the stickiest, gooiest red mud Franklin had ever seen.

Daddy, too, used a walking stick. Soon his long, navy blue pants were splattered at the cuffs with red mud stains. They slipped and slopped along, splashing through springs and creeks.

"Here's a bush you need to see," Pedro said, leading them from the highway to study it. Franklin was glad for a rest. Daddy readjusted the white bucket hat on his head and pulled a red bandanna from his pocket to wipe his flushed face. He lowered his backpack to the ground.

"See how this bush is covered with ants?" With his machete Pedro chopped off a green branch. Franklin stepped up close for a look. The whole inside of the branch was hollow, swarming with ants.

"The Azteca ants sting. Birds won't go near this bush."

They tramped on down the jungle highway. Pedro pointed out the basket tree. "Our ladies use the vine, split it and weave it," he explained. "If they want a darker color, they scrape it and the vine darkens."

Pedro showed them the majestic mahogany tree and the cahoon, the leaves of which natives use to thatch the roofs of their huts. "One roof lasts about five years," he said. "A load of leaves is very heavy, but still the natives "back" them, carrying them all the way to the village."

Some places along the highway, the jungle canopy became so thick it nearly blocked out the bright noon sunlight. Howler monkeys swung from high in the tree tops, screaming to each other. Often Franklin lagged behind the men. Craning his neck, he peered up into a giant canopy tree with liana wrapped like a wide wooden band all the way around its bare trunk up to the leafy branches overhead.

When they arrived at a "plantation," Franklin thought it looked like an overgrown field of weeds and tree stumps. As they walked across the field, Pedro explained how the farmers plant corn.

"To clear a plantation in the jungle, the men form a long row and clear the bush with their machetes. After the brush dries, we burn it. Then it is ready to plant." Sharpening a stick

about the size of a garden hoe handle, he poked a hole in the ground. "We do this all over the field. Four to seven seeds are dropped into a hole and are covered. The seeds sprout and grow. Then we have corn."

Leaving the cleared land, they entered the jungle again. They followed Pedro single file as he cleared the path with his machete. Once he stopped them with his raised hand. An old cahoon leaf lay in the path. Cautiously he approached it. With the tip of the machete he lifted it away. "Snakes like to hide under these old, deteriorating leaves. We must always be careful," he explained.

They were following the stream as it wound round in the jungle. Pedro cocked his head. "I think I hear a partridge!" he exclaimed. "If we'd be going home, I'd go after it. But we are nearly at San Jose village. Before we arrive I will show you yet one more thing."

That was when Pedro introduced Franklin to what he thought was the most fascinating thing in the jungle.

CHAPTER  7

Xavier Clemente
Tells His Story

With his machete Pedro whacked off a piece of brown vine about four feet long and as thick as Franklin's wrist. Lifting up one end, he held the other end just above his mouth as water poured from it.

"You want to try it, yes?"

Franklin tilted his head, opened his mouth, and was surprised

by the refreshing drink from such a strange place. *Water. From a vine.* Daddy drank also.

"It's amazing how much water that vine holds," Daddy said, stepping back to examine the mass of vines near the ground.

"The secret is in making two quick cuts. Otherwise the water is absorbed again by the roots," Pedro explained.

The jungle thinned and huts

appeared again in the distance. San Jose village spread out at the foot of a hillside. It was probably twice the size of Little Amazon. At the first hut they asked directions to Xavier Clemente's house.

"Go down the path to the first fork," said a toothless woman sitting in the shade of her hut. A goat was tied to a post near a pigpen where an old sow huffed and grunted, nosing in under the fencing wire in the dust. "At the fork stay left and go to the lone store with a Coca Cola sign above the window. Take the path to the right. Go past two coconut trees. Clemente's house is the third one after you cross the log bridge."

Pedro thanked her and the small party moved on. *It's all so primitive here. People live just like the ones at Little Amazon,* Franklin thought. *It's so different from our modern lifestyle in the States.*

About then they arrived at a lime green, Spanish-style house that stood out from the rest of the village huts. Made of stucco and rock, with arched windows, the rectangular structure was a welcome sight to the weary men. They entered the walled Clemente compound by way of the metal gate.

An old, white-haired man in a brown robe greeted them. Franklin recognized him as the same man who had traveled back from Tampico with them in the skiff. "I have been expecting you," he said, inviting them into the cool interior. The home was simply but tastefully decorated. From the foyer they followed Xavier into the living room and sat down in the wicker chairs he indicated. "I hoped my message would bring you, Mathias."

The younger man shook his head. "How do you know my name, sir?" he said, puzzled.

"I will tell you a story, but only after you have had some refreshment." A maid appeared carrying a silver tray with iced glasses of Fanta for each. When she had finished distributing the glasses, she returned with delicious-looking pastries—jam-filled cakes with fancy icing.

"You had no trouble on your way through the jungle?" Xavier asked.

"No, none whatsoever. My friend here knows the land quite well." Daddy smiled at Pedro.

"And you will soon be returning to the States?"

"We plan to leave in two days, if the Lord wills." Daddy spoke gently, but expectantly, inviting their host to explain why he had called them on this mission.

Xavier got up, his sandaled feet slapping the ornate wooden floor. Back and forth he paced, the robe gently swaying with his lithe movements. "I have a son named Jacinto," the old man began. "He is my only son. Years ago a man, an American, came to the city and told him and his friend about Jesus Christ. My son then spoke to me about becoming a Christian. However, there was one problem. My wife and I are Muslim. To convert to Christianity is completely forbidden. Conversion dishonors the family. My son believed the missionary and became a Christian along with his wife.

"At that time we lived in Belize City where I sold my carvings. My wife and I and our friends became very angry. Jacinto's windows were splattered with paint. Bricks were thrown into their garden. Their car was torched. On the street they were kicked, punched, and spat on. My son and his family became prisoners in their own house. Finally we drove them away. I told them to leave and never come back. He and his wife left, weeping."

Pedro, Daddy, and Franklin sat speechless. *How could a man do such things to his own boy?* Back and forth, back and forth paced their host like a man driven.

"Then I began to have torments. Evil thoughts haunted me. I wanted to die. I was so angry that Christianity had stolen my son and robbed me of my two beautiful grandchildren. But I couldn't forget one thing. I could not forget how happy Jacinto and Ramona had become after they believed. Even with all the persecution, the expression on their faces was so peaceful. Jacinto tried to explain it to me, but I wouldn't listen. It made me even angrier. Now I was the one with torments.

"I needed peace. I had to have peace or I knew I'd lose my mind. We moved to San Jose and I built this house. I have become an old man.

"For months now I have been having a dream. A man in white comes and teaches me out of a book that is not the Koran, the Muslim's holy book. If I do as he says, things go well for me. If I don't, things go badly. I have secretly started studying Christianity from books I have bought when I travel with my carvings. They have answered many of my questions.

"Last week the man in white told me to go to Tampico and gave me a vision of an American man. I had small business to carry out so I went. On the way back on the skiff I discovered you, Mathias Van Pelt, were the man in my dream. And you were also the man who led my son Jacinto to Christianity. I know for I asked Antonio, the carver from Little Amazon. He was Jacinto's friend and was with him the day you two met and talked. Antonio hates me for driving him away."

That's why Antonio froze up when I started asking questions about Xavier Clemente, Franklin thought. *Now it makes sense.* Pedro sat sprawled in his chair, arms flung out, bereft of speech. As Franklin watched his father's face, a look of surprise and wonder came over his tanned features.

"Praise God!" Daddy exclaimed, getting to his feet. "It is He who directed us to Little Amazon so you may also find peace."

Xavier stopped his pacing. Taking a small glass urn from the dining room table, he rolled it around and around in his hands. Then he set it down again, too distracted to realize it stood upside down.

"I still have some questions. Perhaps you can guide me? Muslims do not believe that Jesus died on the cross. Nobody killed Him or crucified Him. God is too merciful. I don't believe He'd ever allow enemies to kill such a wonderful prophet."

A glow came over Daddy's face as he said, "Let me get my

Bible out of my backpack."

For the next two hours Daddy and Pedro pored over the scriptures with Xavier, showing him truths from God's Word.

"In Genesis 22, God asks Abraham to offer his son Isaac as a sacrifice on Mt. Moriah in obedience to his command. Why would God ask such a thing of His friend, and just when Abraham was about to kill his son with a knife, an angel stops him? Then God provides a ram? The ram was a substitute for Abraham's son. Could the ram represent Jesus Christ?" Daddy asked.

Xavier nodded. "Yes, maybe so."

"We can look back today, 2,000 years later and see Jesus on the cross, a sacrifice for you and me. In John 1:29 John the Baptist says, "Behold the Lamb of God, which taketh away the sin of the world."

Pedro turned to Isaiah 53. "Read this out loud," he instructed. Xavier responded and falteringly read the entire chapter.

"Who is the prophet talking about?" probed Pedro.

"It is clear," Xavier reflected. "He is talking about *Issa*, the son of Mary."

"That which was written by the prophet Isaiah about the Messiah was fulfilled in Jesus Christ 600 years later," Daddy affirmed.

The men talked on and on. Part of the conversation had been interesting to Franklin, but then his eyes grew heavy from the long tramp. Arranging a pillow to his head, he fell into a deep sleep.

"Franklin." It was Daddy's voice calling him. Stirring, he squinted his eyes. "Are you hungry? Wake up. Supper is being served." Franklin sat up, disoriented for a moment.

"It's too late to travel through the jungle tonight. Xavier has invited us to stay for the night. We'll start back in the morning."

Xavier and his energetic wife extended the finest hospitality to their guests that evening.

Shortly after dawn, Pedro, Daddy, and Franklin started on their way home again. Pedro had promised to send someone from Little Amazon to disciple Xavier and his wife, for she too had become a believer with her husband.

CHAPTER  8

Red Mud
and Raw Coconuts

On the trek back Franklin thought the path seemed stickier, muddier, and more slippery to his weary feet. He was still sore from the hike yesterday. However, his thoughts, more than his feet, demanded his attention.

"Daddy," he said, hurrying his steps to keep up. They had just passed the plantation. "How come missionaries live such exciting lives here in Belize? God . . . He feels so close."

"How do you mean?"

"When people pray, He answers. Like getting the purse back, and praying when the drunks circled the house. God answered my 911 prayer."

"That was really wonderful, Franklin. I'm glad it happened."

"You talked to Jacinto years ago, and he and his wife became Christians. Now also his father and mother. I don't hear people at home talk about God all the time and about what He does. Why, Daddy?"

"That's the exciting thing about being a missionary, Franklin. But miracles don't just happen in Belize. They happen in the United States too—wherever people are sold out to God."

"What do you mean, 'sold out'?"

"Well, as an example, look at missionaries who live intentionally first for God and secondly for the souls of the people they are trying to win. Their goal in a foreign land is not to live comfortably for themselves. It is not to make money. It is not to become a citizen of the land and get involved in that country's activities. Their business is God's work, investing in things that will last forever.

"Sometimes they get lonely, homesick, or discouraged. They can't just run home for the evening. They feel it keenly that they are *very far* from home. This drives them to God who comforts them. When they are in trouble and cry out to God, He sends his angels to deliver them." Daddy slowed his steps to a halt. Pedro, ahead a little ways, moved off the trail to rest under a shade tree.

"Like what He did for us?"

"Yes," Daddy nodded.

"But in the States we use a telephone to call the vet when a calf or a puppy is sick," Franklin said thoughtfully. "If the car slips into the ditch, we call the tow truck with a cell phone. When there's an accident, we call 911. A lot of people pray when they're in big trouble though."

"Personal disaster makes people call on God. In wealthier countries, many people live insulated, secure lives, but are not very involved with God."

"I think I'd rather be a missionary, Daddy," declared Franklin. "It's about the best way to live."

"That's why I brought you down here, son," Daddy grinned, reaching over to ruffle Franklin's hair. "Have you missed the farm much?"

Franklin whacked his hand against his forehead. "Aw, Daddy. Come to think of it, I've hardly given the farm a thought. So much has been happening. The farm seems so far away."

Daddy's voice grew serious. "I don't know what God has in mind for your future, Franklin. But I would feel greatly honored to be the father of a man who is a missionary."

"A 'sold-out' missionary?" Franklin asked.

"Yes, son, an intentional, sold-out missionary for God."

As they neared Little Amazon village, Pedro took them on two side trips. One was to an altar where natives used to offer food and incense to their gods. The second was to the mouth of the creek that flowed by Antonio's place.

In the shade of a tall tree, Pedro cut open two coconuts with his machete and let Franklin and Daddy taste the milk. It looked like clear syrup. Franklin didn't care much for the bland taste.

Would being a missionary mean I'd have to eat raw coconut? Or chocolate-covered grasshoppers? Franklin's thoughts tumbled and mixed with his yawns over a late lunch back at the mission. *I guess when you think about how happy Xavier was after he accepted Jesus into his heart last night, you could avoid thinking about how gross insects taste.*

"You may curl up in the hammock on the porch," Pedro's wife Elena invited, clearing away the rice and beans and lettuce salad from the table. "No need to sleep in that chair."

Mama was folding laundry on the sofa and placing it back into the suitcases. "Yes, Franklin. We don't want you sleepwalking while you work. Take a little nap before you start packing your bags. Daddy says we leave at 2:30 in the morning."

A volleyball game was planned for the evening, but a pouring rain dampened the idea. Still the church young folks wanted to play. So Franklin, Kate, and Max joined them for two rounds in the red mud after the rain stopped.

At the mission house Pedro's family stood for pictures. Then the Van Pelts, and next Garth and Rachel. Kayla and Julie

posed with Kate. Then Julie wanted Franklin and Max to join them. What a wonderful time it had been. Franklin couldn't believe it was so nearly over. *When will we see these nice people again? My, they're just about like family.*

CHAPTER 9

Cold Night Ride
Into the Future

It was a restless night for Franklin. From the darkness, disturbing noises came from just outside the hut. Way in the distance, across the village, he heard pigs squealing and squealing. *What is going on?* he wondered. Kate and Max slept serenely through it all.

Frequently something ran around the guesthouse and a dog outside gave a low growl. Something thumped hard three or four times against the door. Once he thought he heard voices.

Franklin rolled about on the bunk. He plumped his pillow. He rearranged the covers. Nothing helped. Finally he forced himself to lie completely still.

Then Mama was bending over his bed in the darkness. "Franklin, it's time to get up. The skiff will be leaving soon." She called to Max in the bunk above his and then hurried out to rouse Kate. Franklin groaned and looked at the clock. *2:15 a.m. I probably got only an hour and a half of sleep.*

By the dim light of the oil lamp, Franklin, Max, and Kate gathered their belongings. Pedro helped the Van Pelts carry their luggage to the skiff.

After all the village passengers were aboard, the men came carrying one squealing pig after another. They loaded four into the front of the boat. *Four pigs! So that is what all the commotion was about. They were rounding up pigs. And we will be traveling with them!*

The night was still fairly dark. Overhead, a silver moon shone and stars twinkled. Flashes of light from several flashlights illuminated the shadowy men on the bank. Voices called to each other in Kekchi. Franklin understood only a few words.

It was well past four when the skiff began the cold, three-hour trip out to Tampico. Shadowy jungle slipped by as the boat flew over dark water. Without a wind break, cold, damp air came through Franklin's light jacket and made him shiver. Max leaned on Mama's shoulder. "I'm cold," he complained. Kate held her book up to her face. Rachel offered a large towel, but it wasn't enough. The cold still came through.

Franklin gritted his teeth. As hard as he tried, he couldn't keep them from chattering. The relentless cold wind penetrated his body into his bones. He shivered and shook. It was miserable. He repositioned himself, trying to duck down behind the passengers ahead of him. It was no use.

Then he remembered something. "Kate." He poked his sister. "Where's your umbrella?" Rummaging in her bag she produced it for him.

"Yes!" he cheered, popping it open. "O bliss!" Diverted, the wind now moved up and over their heads. Together Franklin and Kate huddled behind the black shield. Mama noticed and found her umbrella too.

After two hours on the river, the sun came up and the air grew warmer. All the passengers perked up when they reached the sea. An hour across the silvery water and the dock at Tampico came into view.

For breakfast the Van Pelts and party ate at a beautiful restaurant Kate said must be the best in town. The only thing on the menu was an order of scrambled eggs with bacon, a deep-fried, half-moon pastry, and orange juice. The decor in the room was pink—so charming and clean compared to all the mud and dirt they had contended with at Little Amazon and on the skiff.

The restaurant was so pleasant it was easy to stay sitting. "Daddy," Franklin said when there was a lull in the conversation. "What happened on the sea that time you almost lost a few passengers? Remember, you said you'd tell me."

Daddy looked across the table at Mama, and Franklin didn't miss the look of warmth that passed between them.

"Well, son, the passengers were friends who had come to visit Garth. When the sea got rough, I prayed that God would save us. I wanted a chance to get acquainted with that pretty, dark-haired lady in pink. God saved us. The lady is your mama," he grinned.

At 3 p.m. the plane lifted again from the town of Tampico, headed for Belize City.

Franklin sat directly behind the pilot. Just as on the first flight, he watched in fascination as the tropical jungle skimmed by beneath them. What a magnificent view!

The loud engine made conversation difficult, giving Franklin time to muse over the past ten days. *Maybe someday I'll come back here*, Franklin thought, remembering his conversation with Daddy. *But first I have to grow up. There are probably a lot of men like Xavier who need a man like Daddy to guide them.* Glancing at Daddy, he realized his father was watching him, a gentle smile playing on his face. Franklin smiled back.

About the Author

Lena Eicher resides in the western hills of Holmes County, Ohio, where she provides spiritual care and a safe haven for women struggling with critical life issues. Lena has written numerous short stories for Sunday school periodicals and self-published one book. Her extensive travels have included trips to Central America and Europe, and in 2000, a three-month stint on the Mercy Ship *Anastasis*, which began in Holland and ended in Benin, Africa. Although born and raised in Holmes County, Lena spent 20 years of her adult life in Grantsville, Maryland, where she traveled weekends with the Mountain Anthems choir. She returned to her native home in 2008.